For String, Ick-Stick, Nemo, Dopus-Manopus, Int, Tiny, and my best friend, Bug

—J. H.

For Seth

—P. H.

SIMON & SCHUSTER BOOKS FOR YOUNG READERS
An imprint of Simon & Schuster Children's Publishing Division
1230 Avenue of the Americas, New York, New York 10020

Book design by Paula Winicur
The text of this book is set in Joanna.
The illustrations are rendered in watercolor.

Printed in Hong Kong
2 4 6 8 10 9 7 5 3 1

Library of Congress Cataloging-in-Publication Data
Huling, Jan.
Puss in cowboy boots / Jan Huling ; illustrated by Phil Huling. — 1st ed.
p. cm.
Summary: Set in Texas, a retelling of the fairy tale in which a clever cat wins for his master a fortune and a wealthy and talented bride.
ISBN 0-689-83119-6
[1. Fairy tales. 2. Folklore—France.] I. Huling, Phil, ill. II. Title.
PZ8.H875Pu 2000
[398.2]—dc21
99-14498

BY

JAN HULING

PICTURES BY PHIL HULING

SIMON & SCHUSTER BOOKS FOR YOUNG READERS
New York • London • Toronto • Sydney • Singapore

Once upon a time deep in the wilds of Texas, there was a rodeo clown who went by the name of Clem. Now ol' Clem had three boys and not much else. Just his old pickup truck, his clown suit, and a scraggly old tomcat who went by the name of Puss.

One day ol' Clem up and kicked the bucket.

Now, like I said, Clem didn't have much stuff, and his boys wanted something to remember him by.

So the oldest got his first choice, which was that beat-up, rusty old pickup truck. "It ain't much," he said, "but I reckon it'll get me around."

The middle boy took the next choice, which was his pa's old clown suit. "It ain't much," he said, "but I reckon I can make a living in it."

The third son got what was left: old Puss. "It ain't much," he said, "but . . . it ain't much."

So Dan (that was this youngest fella's name, Dan), he takes his inheritance and sets off down the road, though he doesn't know where to. Finally he gets tired of wandering around and sits himself down to make a plan.

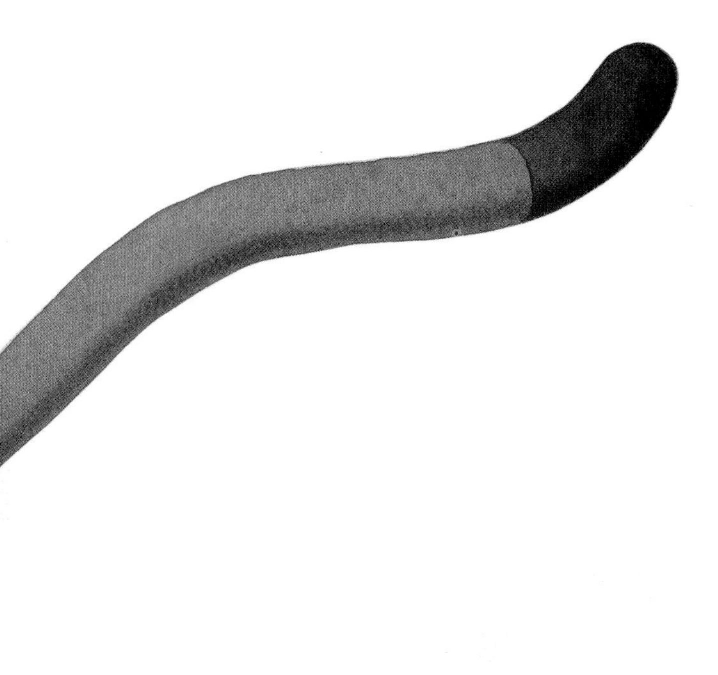

S
6
207
EXAS

"Well, I'll be danged," he said, "if this don't just beat all! Here I am in the biggest, the richest, the most powerful state in the Union, and all I got to show for myself is this dang cat! More trouble than it's worth. Heck, after I've turned him into a pot o' three-alarm chili and tanned his hide for a hatband, I won't have nothin'!"

Now old Puss was sittin' back just takin' all this in, and he didn't warm to the idea of being served up with a side o' beans. So he says, "Whoa there! Just hold on a dad-burned minute, boy! I want you to take a good long look at these old bones and think about what a puny, no-account bowl o' red I'd make! Why, I ain't much more 'n fur and bones, and as far as a hatband . . ."

"All right, all right, I get the idea," says Dan. "You don't look much tastier than a piece of gristle in a cold mud pie anyhow. But you ain't doin' me no good as it is. Why don't you just hit the road, pardner, and we'll say adios."

"Now, hold your horses there, son! I ain't gonna up and leave you high and dry. I'll tell you what. You go on and get me a pair of cowboy boots and an old burlap sack. I got me a plan that's gonna make you gladder than a mosquito at a blood bank and will keep me in sardines and sweet cream for life!"

That was all the cat had to say, and Dan, figuring he had nothin' left to lose, went into town and got that cat a sack and the purdiest pair of red snakeskin cowboy boots ever worn by man or feline.

Now Puss really did have a plan, or at least part of one, which was way more plan than Dan had! So he put on his boots, grabbed his sack, and headed off to the woods. Back in his less scraggly days he'd been a champion mouser and he figured he still had a trick or two up his sleeve. So he found some grain and tossed it into his sack. Then he propped it open and hunkered down behind an old tree stump and commenced to wait.

Wasn't long before a big ol' wild turkey came pokin' around looking for his supper. "Well, what have we got here?" gobbled this none-too-bright bird. "I reckon I got me a secret admirer gone and left me a treat! Now ain't that nice? I'll just have a little ol' taste . . ." And when he got himself way on into that bag, Puss whipped it closed before ol' Wild Bill Turkey could say yee-ha!

Puss threw the sack, with the turkey in it, over his shoulder and hightailed it into the big city and straight to the office of the biggest, the richest, and the most powerful oilman in the state of Texas. He shot straight on in and said, "Mister, I'm here with a little ol' gift from Rancher Dan, the biggest, the richest, and the most powerful rancher in all of the Lone Star State!"

Mr. Patoot (that was his name, Mr. Patoot), he was so surprised and impressed by that cat's audacity (not to mention his boots!) that he laughed out loud. "Why, looky here!" he says. "A wild turkey! Why, I remember huntin' these with my pa when I was no bigger than a frog's hair. Ma used to cook 'em up with a truckload of chilies—now that's good eatin'! I thank you kindly, little buddy, and Rancher Dan, too (whoever he is!)." Puss left that office grinning like a bear in a beehive. He reckoned his plan was off to a bang-up start.

Couple days later, Puss bagged an o'possum much the same way as he did that turkey and, again, scooted on into Mr. Patoot's office. "Mister, I'm here with another little ol' gift from Rancher Dan, the biggest, the richest, and the most powerful rancher in all of the Lone Star State!"

Well now, that wild turkey stew had gone down so nice that Mr. Patoot was delighted to see old Puss back again with another sack of something. When he saw it was an o'possum, he let out a whoop! "Puss, you and Rancher Dan do know the way to this country boy's heart! Why, I can almost smell Ma's possum pie a-bakin'," he said, wiping a tear from his eye. "You tell Rancher Dan I'm much obliged!"

Now this went on for a couple of months, and it got so that Mr. Patoot looked forward to Puss's visits and especially to those gifts that brought him happy memories of his Texas boyhood.

After a time Puss found out that Mr. Patoot's daughter, Rosie-May, was back home from the art school she went to in New York City and that she and her daddy were planning a picnic out in the country. So Puss said to Dan, "Boy, you do as I say and see if you don't end up as lucky as a fish in a flood. Now I want you to strip down to your Skivvies and go for a little swim in this here creek by the road."

Dan did as he was told even though he didn't have a clue as to what was going on. Pretty soon Puss saw Mr. Patoot's big ol' limo coming over the hill, and he commenced to yelling, "Help! Help! Rancher Dan is drowning!" and he flagged down the car. Mr. Patoot recognized Puss and told his driver to jump into that creek and rescue Rancher Dan. So while old Dan was being dragged out of the water, Puss went over to Mr. Patoot and explained, "It was the dangest thing! We were drivin' along, just enjoying this fine day, when some rascals stopped us, stole Rancher Dan's fine clothes, and threw him in the creek! Then they took the dang car! Why, it's a miracle you came along when you did!"

So Mr. Patoot and Rosie-May decided that this was as good a place as any for a picnic and asked Puss and the nearly nekked Rancher Dan to join them while Mr. Patoot's driver headed into town to pick up some new duds for Dan. Everybody liked this idea, 'specially Rosie-May, who'd brought her sketchbook and found Dan to be a good model (and easy on the eyes to boot). Dan was impressed, seeing as he'd never met a real artist before (and a purdy one at that). Before you knew it, those two young folks had taken a shine to each other.

Wasn't too long before Mr. Patoot's driver was back with a fine new set of clothes, shiny new cowboy boots, and a ten-gallon hat to top it all off. Now all dressed up, Dan looked like a million bucks, and Mr. Patoot suggested that they all take a ride together. "You all go along," said Puss. "I've got some chores to see to, so I'll meet up with y'all later."

So Puss went on ahead and came to a field with more cattle grazing on it than he could count, and he yelled to the cowboys tending the cattle, "Hey there! I was wondering if y'all could help me out. You tell the fella in the limo that these here cattle belong to Rancher Dan, and if you do, you can come to the shindig he's having tonight—best dang bar-be-que you ever sunk your teeth into!" The cowboys said they would, and Puss ran on ahead.

Before too long, Mr. Patoot's limo drove up, and Mr. Patoot rolled down the window to ask the cowboys who owned all those head of cattle. "Why, Rancher Dan calls these cattle his," said the cowboys, "and he makes a mean bar-be-que, too!" they added, and commenced to whooping and yee-ha-ing and hollering, as cowboys are inclined to do, until the limo drove away.

Next, Puss saw a field of some fifty-odd oil rigs just pumping away, and he yelled out to the workers, "Hey there! I was wondering if y'all could help me out. You tell the fella in the limo that this here oil belongs to Rancher Dan, and if you do, you can come to the shindig he's having tonight—best dang bar-be-que you ever sunk your teeth into!" So they said okay, and Puss ran on ahead.

Sure enough, Mr. Patoot's limo pulled up, and Mr. Patoot called out to the folks doing the drilling to ask who owned all that oil. "That would be old Rancher Dan," they said, "and that lucky cuss knows his way around a bar-be-que pit, that's for sure!" and with that they commenced to laughing and slapping their knees until the limo drove away.

"Well, I'll be danged, Dan," said Mr. Patoot, "if this ain't the biggest, the richest, and the most powerful ranch in all of Texas! And you sure keep your hired hands happy!"

"Uh, yep, I reckon so," replied Dan, still clueless as to what was going on. And on it went, past trout stream and wheat field, everyone claiming to be working for Rancher Dan and praising his bar-be-que skills.

REMEMBER
the
ALAMO

Finally Puss came to a great big, beautiful ranch house that belonged to a great big, ugly ogre. He was the biggest, the meanest, the cattle-rustlingest, oil-guzzlingest outlaw of an ogre in the world, and what's more—he knew magic! Now this here ogre had used all of that badness and meanness and magic to lay claim to all of that countryside that Mr. Patoot and the others were passing through. Puss, knowing all about this ogre, walked himself right on up to the door and rang the bell.

Pretty soon he found himself sitting face-to-face with that ol' ogre and said to him, "Folks 'round here say you can change yourself into any old thing you have a mind to. But then, you know how folks talk."

"So you think it's just talk, do you?" the ogre replied, and right there turned himself into a Texas twister! Now you can imagine the commotion a tornado would cause inside a house, and Puss was so scared he lit on out the window and up onto the roof.

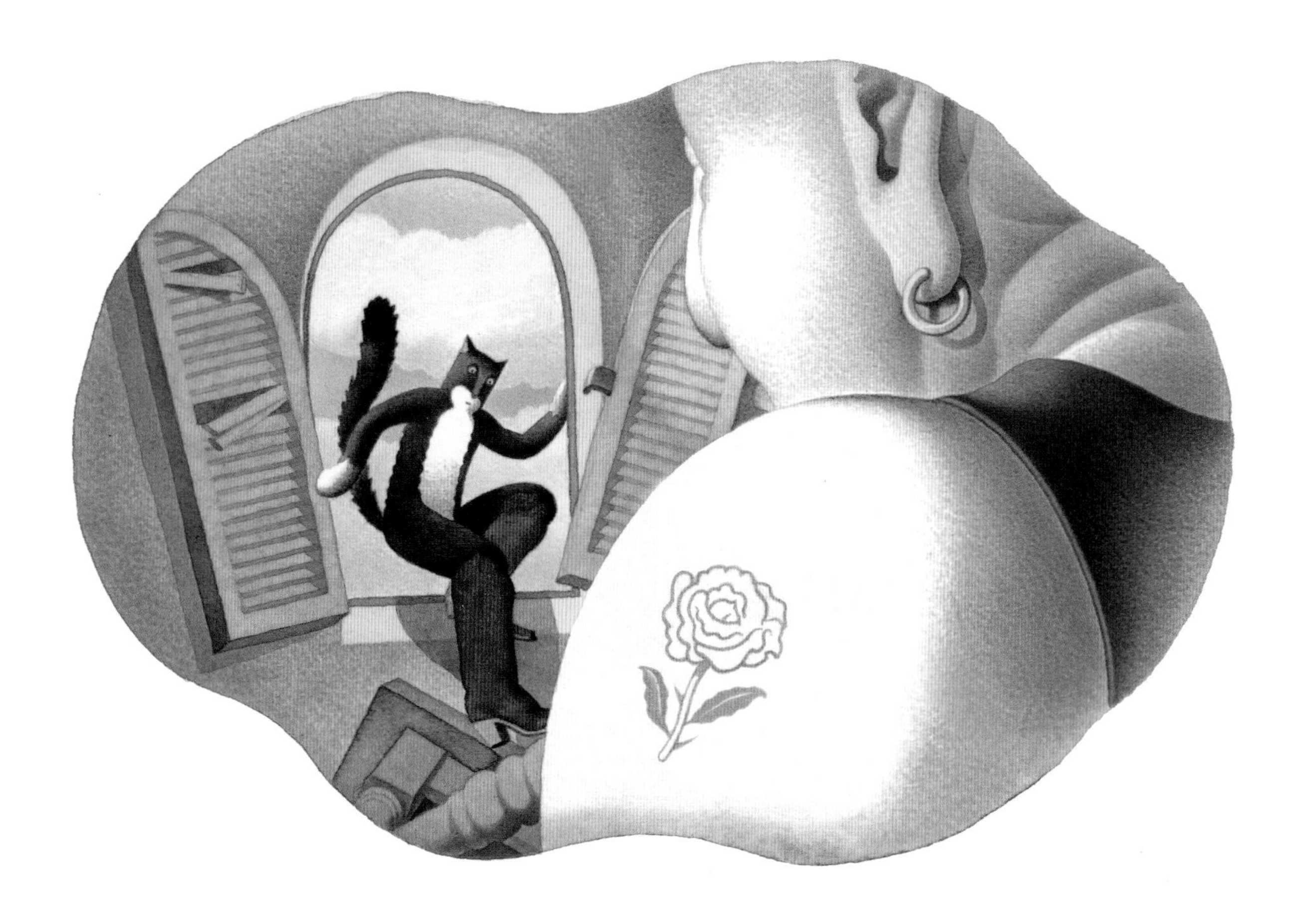

After a while, when things calmed down, Puss climbed back inside and said, "Well, oooo-eeee, Mr. Ogre, I reckon those folks were right! Y'all sure 'nuff gave me a start! But I don't guess you could turn your big ol' self into something tiny, could you? Say, a little bitty old prairie mouse or something, huh?"

"You don't guess I could? You just watch this!" said the ogre, and then he disappeared. Puss looked down at the floor and saw a tiny little prairie mouse sittin' there lookin' all proud of itself. Puss pounced on it, sprinkled it with cayenne pepper, and gobbled it down!

Right about then, Mr. Patoot's limo pulled up to the ranch, and Puss ran outside to meet it. "Welcome to Rancher Dan's spread!" he called out as he opened the limo door.

"Well, I'll be dingdong danged, Dan!" declared Mr. Patoot. "Why, I'm speechless, boy, and that's a rare state for a Texan to be in, let me tell you!" Rosie-May was pretty impressed, too, but not so much by the ranch as by the rancher, who seemed just as simple and down-to-earth as he was rich.

That night Rancher Dan threw a shindig the likes of which had never been seen in all the state of Texas. Why, he served up possum pie and wild turkey stew and all manner of bar-be-que, which all the folks who worked on the ranch agreed was the best dang bar-be-que they'd ever sunk their teeth into! There were fireworks and games and music, and in the middle of a Texas two-step, Rosie-May promised Dan that she'd be his bride! It was a memorable night!

And where was Puss while all this hootin' and hollerin' was going on? Why, after his supper of sardines and sweet cream, he took off those good ol' cowboy boots, found the biggest, the richest, and the softest pillow on the ranch, and took a nap.